Take Care of Millie

by Jessie Redding Hull

Edited by Wendy Stein

Illustrated by Sandra Gould
Cover by Sally Rubadeau

sundown books

New Readers Press ● *Syracuse, New York*

*To Richard Gotsch, the first principal of my
teaching years in the Affton School District,
St. Louis County, Missouri*

© 1980
New Readers Press
Publishing Division of Laubach Literacy International
Box 131, Syracuse, New York 13210

Printed in the United States of America

9 8 7 6 5 4 3 2

Chapter 1

Flowers surrounded the casket of George C. Nelson. A woman in black leaned over the body. Millie Nelson studied her husband's features for the last time. She touched his face.

"Life's going to be strange without you," she said. "Nobody to cook for. No dirty socks. No yelling, 'Bring me a beer.' No snoring or cold feet at night. Even the bad stuff, George. They say you miss a headache if you've had it long enough. That's the way it was with us. Not that we were headaches, but—"

Millie's face was drawn with sorrow. Her 68 years seemed 75. Tears made a path along the wrinkles under her eyes.

"I'll always love you, George," she whispered as she gently kissed the lifeless lips.

Millie's daughter, Jan, appeared at the doorway.

"The undertaker is waiting to take Dad to the cemetery, Mom," Jan said. "All those people who came to the service—they're in their cars, waiting."

"Don't you want to say another goodbye to your father, Jan dear? He looks so peaceful lying there."

For a moment, Jan became patient. Gently, but firmly, she took her mother by the arm.

"It's time to go, Mom," she said as she led her mother from the room.

"Seems a shame that the world's in such a hurry all the time." Millie sighed as she looked back.

Janet Beal glanced back at her husband. He trailed two steps behind. Why was he no help? She had to decide everything. Without her father, her mother couldn't manage alone. Jan was going to insist that her mother move in with them. Fred had said that Millie was welcome to move in. But he wasn't going to push her.

As they stepped outside, a brisk fall breeze brushed by them. The widow's warm tears turned into icy wetness. Millie straightened her hat. She centered it over her short, white, tightly curled hair.

What a lovely service, Millie thought. It was nice of Pastor Stevens to say all those wonderful things about George. Especially since George had shouted at the pastor last time they were together. He said the church was wasting his money. Oh well, Millie reflected, when a man dies you forget all those little problems.

She smiled as she thought of the candy George had brought her when Jan was born. The hospital said that nursing mothers shouldn't eat chocolate. So George ate it—and kept telling her how good it was!

Yes, it had been a comfortable 40 years with George.

* * * *

Millie wanted Jan and Fred to go home after the services. Jan insisted that Millie should not be alone. Fred went home. But Jan stayed overnight.

"Mother, Fred and I want you to move in with us. When do you think you'll be ready?"

"Jan, I can't do that."

"Of course you can. We want you, and you need us, Mom."

The phone rang. It was for Jan. Millie was relieved to drop the subject. She was tired of Jan's pushing. Sure, George had been pushy. But he was her husband. A daughter shouldn't be that way.

* * * *

That night, the bed seemed wrong. George's big, clumsy body should be weighing down the side next to her. Once they had promised, "Till death do us part." But death wasn't real. George should be there always. She missed the cold feet, snoring, and all. Inside her, there was an emptiness.

Millie reached over and touched the vacant half of the bed. "Half of me is in the grave," she murmured.

Hours passed. Millie couldn't sleep.

Quietly, she put on her slippers and robe. She felt her way along the hall—a light might wake Jan. Millie tiptoed down the stairs.

In the kitchen, she fumbled for the light switch. Then, she took out the note cards.

The cards from the flowers were in a box on the table. Where to start? Who should she thank first? And what to say? "Thank you" didn't seem enough. "Thank you for thinking of us in our time of sorrow?" No, it was important to say something special to each person.

"Mother, is that you?"

Millie didn't answer. She was angry that her quiet was gone.

"Mother, what are you doing?"

"You can see what I'm doing," Millie said.

"But it's two o'clock."

"I couldn't sleep."

"The doctor should have given you some pills," Jan said.

"Jan, you know I don't take sleeping pills." Millie kept on writing without looking up.

"Now, get back to bed, Mother. You must get some rest."

Millie went back to bed.

"What can I do, George?" she wept. "She keeps pushing me. I don't want to hurt her, but—"

"Oh God," she sobbed. She was letting go of the stress of the day. The crowd. The funeral. Jan's orders. And why was Jan insisting that she give up her home? To lose George was sorrow enough.

Thoughts of the old days soon filled her mind. Then, the sweetness of a time long ago with a smiling husband and a happy baby put Millie to sleep.

Chapter 2

Millie awoke to find Jan standing by the bed.

"Don't get up, Mom. You need your rest."

As Millie sat up, Jan straightened the covers around her.

"Don't move. I have a surprise for you." Jan left the room. She quickly returned with a tray.

"How's this for service?" Jan beamed as she presented the tray to Millie.

"It's beautiful." Tears came to Millie's eyes. She saw George in Jan's large brown eyes.

"You shouldn't have gone to all that trouble." Millie looked at the orange juice, pancakes, and coffee. Though she would rather have had her usual toast and coffee, she was touched by Jan's offering.

Smiling, Jan leaned over. Millie kissed her cheek. Then Millie hurried to finish her breakfast.

"Hey, slow down," Jan said.

"I want to get the dishes back to the people who sent food, and—"

"Done," Jan said. She pulled up a chair and sat by her mother's bed. "The names were on everything. I washed them and returned them this morning."

"Thank you, dear." Millie tried to sound grateful. It was a little thing, but she really had wanted to do it herself. She especially wanted to talk with Gertrude. How could a friend do so much?

Gertrude had stayed with her at the funeral home. A year ago, Gertrude had lost her husband. She knew the feeling.

"I have errands downtown, Mom. Will you be OK while I'm gone?" Jan picked up the empty food tray.

"If I don't die from overeating," Millie joked. The very idea, she thought. I don't need a nursemaid.

Jan left. Millie was finally alone. She felt a sweet sadness in warm memories.

She knew that George was gone. Yet, as she reached for the blue pantsuit, she felt him complain.

"Millie, women shouldn't go around dressed like men."

The day after he's in the ground. Would I dare? She thought for a moment. Then, she put the outfit back in the closet.

Again, she reached for the pantsuit. But again, she changed her mind. She finally put on the green housedress.

Downstairs, the odor of stew floated from the slow cooker. Even dinner had been taken care of. There was nothing left to do.

She decided to visit Gertrude. But as she reached for her coat, the doorbell rang. Millie froze. She didn't want to talk with the lawyer about the will today.

The door opened. "Yoo-hoo. Anybody home?" Gertrude popped in.

Millie sighed with relief. "I was just getting ready to go over to your place."

The two women sat down on the overstuffed sofa and talked.

"You knew George was dying. With Ned, it was like a lightning bolt," Gertrude said.

Millie shook her head. "Death is death. It's always a shock."

"How are you feeling, Millie? I mean, really?"

"I don't know. He did suffer. But death is a thing you can't prepare for."

"Time heals," Gertrude said. "I still think of our mountain vacation. It was the week before Ned died. It's like yesterday. But the day he died—I can hardly think of what happened. My mind has blanked out the bad."

"Did you ever get guilt feelings?"

"About what?" Gertrude asked.

"Wanting to do things you know he wouldn't like. Only this morning, I reached for that pantsuit George hates." She paused. "I mean hated. I almost wore it."

Gertrude laughed. "Remember how Ned hated anything yellow?" Gertrude was wearing a bright yellow dress.

Millie got out her photo album. The room filled with tears and laughter as the old friends remembered the past. Then Jan came home.

"Hello, Mrs. Brown. Oh, Mother, put those pictures away. Looking back will only upset you."

"I'd better be going." Gertrude was angered by Jan's remark.

"Must you leave so soon?" Millie asked. She walked Gertrude to the door.

When Millie returned, Jan was sitting on the sofa. She was holding a picture that had fallen from the album. Her hands shook as she stared at the picture. Millie sat down beside her daughter.

"That's you on your fourth birthday. Remember?"

"On Daddy's lap," Jan whispered.

"And holding your birthday doll. You loved it so."

Jan was shaking. She looked up in time to see Millie wiping away a tear.

"I'll put it away, Mother. It's making you cry."

"There's nothing wrong with crying, dear."

Jan stared at the picture again. "You're right. It's good to cry. The trouble is—I can't. Daddy meant so much to me. When I feel like crying, my insides are knots. I can't cry. I just feel sick."

Millie put her arm around Jan to comfort her. Still shaking, Jan spoke. "I got a lot done in a short time today."

Her grief is so bottled up, Millie thought. She can't let it out.

"I talked with the lawyer. We won't be able to sell the house until everything's settled," Jan said. "That will be months."

"Jan, I don't want to sell the house!"

"Oh Mom, you don't want to stay here by yourself! This place has three bedrooms. It's just too big."

Millie let the subject drop.

At five o'clock, Fred joined them for dinner. Again, Jan brought up the subject of the house.

"I can't move in with you. You're crowded now in that apartment," Millie said.

"We have two bedrooms," Jan answered.

"That other room belongs to a baby," Millie insisted.

"Having a baby can wait, Mother." Jan spoke through clenched teeth.

But how long, Millie thought. Jan was already in her thirties. She'd been married six years. She'd been using that other bedroom—the one for the baby—as an art studio. Her paintings were nice. But a career couldn't be as important as a baby.

"Mom, you're always welcome with us. But you make up your own mind," Fred said.

Millie was truly happy when Fred insisted on taking Jan home.

"Your mother needs time to think things over," Fred said. "Besides, I miss you."

* * * *

The next few days were almost peaceful. Millie sorted through George's clothes. And Jan called five times a day to complain about the way Millie was doing things.

"Mother, you *gave* the clothes away? We could have had a garage sale."

"A man's last kindness is his clothing being given to the poor," Millie said.

Jan couldn't argue with that.

George had willed almost everything to Millie. With the pension and their savings, she would be comfortable—if she was careful. Jan was named to handle the estate.

If it weren't for a daughter, a lawyer, and red tape, I could survive death, Millie thought. Sometimes she worried about Jan. And sometimes she wanted to take the phone off the hook.

During the week that followed, Gertrude and God were Millie's comfort.

"Jan can't tell you where to live, Millie." Gertrude told Millie to hold fast.

"I love my home. I'm going to stay here until I die," Millie declared.

Chapter 3

Three weeks later, the things for storage were loaded into a van.

Gertrude came up the walk. She wiped away a tear. "You're really going," she said sadly.

"Seemed the best thing to do," Millie said.

"Jan has been pushing you, Millie."

"Not really, Gertrude. But I *am* worried about her. She's so tense since George passed away. Fred says Jan hasn't cried. She doesn't talk about her father at all."

"And you think moving in with her will make a difference?" Gertrude asked. "What about *you*, Millie Nelson? Your friends are here in the old neighborhood."

"Jan'll have one less concern. George put an awful

burden on her, leaving her in charge of things. And he messed up last year's taxes. She won't let Fred help. Doesn't trust the lawyer. Has to do it all herself."

"I wish you weren't going," Gertrude sighed. Millie didn't seem to hear, though.

"And Gertrude, three bedrooms *is* a lot for someone who doesn't like to clean. I was married to George, not the house."

"I still think Jan pushed you," Gertrude answered.

"No, really. I decided it myself. And I knew I was right when the real estate agent brought around those nice young renters."

"You haven't a mean bone in your body, Millie Nelson."

"You'll love Annie and Bill."

"It just doesn't seem right," Gertrude said. "We'll miss you around here." The two women hugged each other.

"Now, Gertrude, don't you go and get tears all over my good pantsuit."

A horn sounded. Fred pulled up in the Dodge. Jan, who was helping her mother pack, rushed out of the house.

"I wish she wouldn't be so nervous," Millie thought out loud.

"Fred, you're just in time," Jan said. "I'm going to make one last check." Then Jan saw Gertrude.

"Oh, Mrs. Brown," she said cheerfully. "Please come to see us. The N bus stops right outside our apartment building."

"Thank you, dear." Gertrude was polite, but she was thinking other thoughts.

"Do we have everything, Mom?" Fred asked as he helped Millie into the car.

"I hope so," Millie sighed. "Goodbye, Gertrude. I'll see you soon."

Millie watched her friend cross the street. She was glad Gertrude didn't look back. If she had, they both would have cried.

Jan rushed out. "All ready. Let's go," she said brightly.

"I-I have to go back in. It'll just take a minute." Millie didn't know why, but she had to take one last look.

"I'll go with you," Jan said. She was afraid her mother would leave a light on, or not lock the door.

"Janet!" Fred spoke sharply. "Your mother can go into her own house by herself."

Fred sensed Millie's feelings. Walls are not just walls. When they've sheltered you for 35 years, they're friends.

Millie turned the key and walked in. All was quiet—except for the old clock. George had set that clock every Sunday at seven a.m. for almost 40 years.

And she had forgotten to take it! Maybe she should leave it for her young renters. Then she decided to ask Fred to come back for it another day—Jan was already so impatient.

The kitchen seemed empty. The table was there . . . and the chairs. But the spice rack was gone from the wall and the trusty old coffee pot was packed away.

Millie didn't go upstairs. If she didn't leave now, she couldn't leave at all. Besides, Jan would come after her if she didn't hurry.

For a while, it was a quiet ride.

Finally, Fred spoke. "Remember that Hawaii trip for highest sales?"

"Yes," Jan said.

"Well, honey, it looks as though I might have it. I'm tied with two others now."

"But we couldn't go," Jan said.

"Why not?" he asked.

Jan made a shushing sound.

"Don't stay home because of me," Millie said. "That would really upset me."

"Mother, I couldn't leave you just two weeks after you move in."

"You most certainly could," Millie said.

"Take it easy. I haven't won the trip yet," Fred laughed.

* * * *

At Jan and Fred's, Millie's room was small. But it had a window overlooking the park.

Millie was glad Fred had brought over her big

rocker last week. It was nice to sit and look at the park. So many people—she wondered about all of them.

"Mom, won't you join us?" Jan called from the next room.

"No thank you, dear. I'll just rest."

"Of course. It's been a big day."

Millie knew the football game was on. But she could take or leave football—and TV.

The rocker by the window was like a TV on the world. It was something that she liked. Jan had never talked of neighbors. She was always busy with her paintings. She probably hadn't met many people.

* * * *

Settling between the sheets that night, Millie missed her own bed. George was gone. The house was gone. Her bed was gone. It was a whole new life. But tomorrow she would visit the park and meet some people. It *could* be a good life.

"I miss you, George," she whispered. Then, after much tossing and turning, she finally fell asleep.

Chapter 4

When daylight streamed through the window, Millie couldn't remember sleeping. The room was strange. She wondered how long it would take to feel at home.

Careful not to wake anyone, she dressed. Then, she sat by the window and watched floating leaves dot the earth.

"Leaf-raking time again. George sure would grumble if he were here," she said to herself as she rocked.

Branches waved gently as the wind stripped them of their leaves. The gold and red leaves danced in the sunlight. Soon the trees would be bare. Then winter would dress them with glittering ice and snow.

Seasons come and go. There's a season for everything, she thought. When George was alive, she was needed. At this hour, she would have been busy fixing breakfast.

Was this the fall of her time? But there was no gentle wind to take her away.

In the park, a young couple strolled hand in hand. They paused and kissed. Their outlines were shadowed by a towering oak.

To be young and have somebody. Millie wiped away a tear as she thought of young lovers of long ago. For a moment, she felt the past . . . a walk in the park . . . George holding her hand . . . a tender kiss. The Lord meant for people to be in twos. But what happens when the Lord takes half the pair?

The smell of bacon floated from the kitchen. Millie started to stand up then sat down again.

I'll stay out of the way, she thought.

She heard whispers from the kitchen. Nobody called her to breakfast. They think I'm asleep, she thought.

All she wanted was toast and coffee. Then she remembered there was a little coffee shop down the street.

Millie slipped on a coat and tiptoed out. She closed the door behind her without a sound. She wasn't sneaking out. But she worried that Jan would be upset. She hoped she'd be back before she was missed.

At the coffee shop, Millie ordered her toast and coffee. But cigar smoke formed a thick screen in the shop. It made her ill. She didn't enjoy her breakfast. She quickly paid her bill and left.

The cool wind felt good on her cheeks. She loved the smells of fall. Maybe the wind would whip the stink of cigar smoke from her clothing.

She knew she should hurry home. But the air refreshed her. The park was across the street. She crossed the street and sat on a bench. If only she had brought her knitting.

A group of children passed on their way to school. "Hi, lady," a boy called out. The others giggled.

"Good morning, children," Millie said. But they were running across the grass and didn't hear her.

Her peace was soon broken by another voice. "Mother, what on earth are you doing here?" When Jan was angry, her firmly set chin looked like her father's.

"I'm enjoying a lovely fall day, dear. Relax and join me. It'll do you good."

"Relax in a city park at nine in the morning, Mother?"

On the way back to the apartment, Jan kept talking about muggers and rapists. Millie said nothing.

Jan was even more upset about the breakfast in the coffee shop.

"Mother, what if my friends hear that you ate at that grease joint? They'll think I don't take care of you."

Now Millie's insides were in knots too. She felt like yelling, "I can take care of myself!" But still she said nothing.

* * * *

For the rest of the morning, Millie knitted by the window. She heard the sounds of clattering dishes and nervous footsteps as Jan did her chores. Then Jan worked on a painting. Because Millie had moved in, Jan had moved her studio to a corner of the kitchen.

Millie enjoyed the world outside her window. A woman older than Millie was feeding the birds. There was a large rip in the woman's coat sleeve. Stringy strands of gray hair stuck out from the woman's scarf. She stroked a pigeon as it ate from her hand.

Millie wanted to hurry down to the park and meet the bird woman. But she thought of Jan and rocked harder.

Just then, Jan poked her head in the door. "Mother, you ought to put a light on if you're going to work." Millie turned on the light. It reflected on the glass. Now it was harder to see outside.

"What are you making, Mom?" Jan touched the thick cable knit.

Millie shrugged her shoulders. "It could be a blanket for a baby—if there was a baby to give it to."

"Don't start that, Mother," Jan said angrily. She quickly turned and left the room. Millie heard her daughter slamming paint brushes and canvases around in the kitchen.

Jan fixed a fast supper that night. She had been invited to show her paintings at City College. She was going there to set up.

Jan had left orders to leave the dishes for her. But after she left, Fred and Millie washed them.

"Things aren't working out the way I hoped." Millie sighed as she handed Fred a dish to dry.

"Jan made it rough today?"

"I thought my being here would reduce her worries. But I'm making things worse. She gets so angry at every little thing I say or do."

"Nonsense, Mom. The trouble is, we're tiptoeing around a time bomb. I'm not sure what to do. But maybe we should just be ourselves instead of walking on eggshells."

They both had noticed a change in Jan's paintings. She used to use sunny colors, yellows and oranges. Now she used only dark shades. And that worried them.

Fred told Millie that he hoped to win the trip to Hawaii. "It might be just what she needs," he said.

"Even if you don't win, dear, you could go there on vacation. With living here, I'll have extra money to help you," Millie told her son-in-law.

"Jan wouldn't stand for that, Mom. And I won't either. But if I win, I think she'll go."

****

The days that followed were quiet. Sitting in the chair by the window didn't cause any trouble. Every day, Millie saw the young lovers. Except for one very cold day, she saw the bird woman. Sometimes there were joggers. A young woman police officer patrolled the park. And every noon, Millie saw office workers sitting on the benches and eating their lunches.

People moved with grace in the pattern of life. As Millie rocked and knitted, she pretended to join the people in the park. Sometimes, she pretended George was there, too.

Everything she had done for Jan as a child, Jan did for her now—and more. As a child, Jan had freedom. Sure, Millie had worried about the first bike . . . the first date . . . the first times she drove. But she had let go of her daughter when the time came.

Love between Millie and Jan was strong. But now it was a hurting thing. They were both choking back feelings. Jan was tense, nervous, bossy. Millie hid her feelings because she didn't want Jan to get more upset and tense.

Being told what to do wasn't new to Millie. George had ruled the roost during their marriage. So many times she had denied her own feelings and given in to him. And now it was Jan.

This can't be the Lord's will, Millie thought. Once Jan is feeling better, I'll—She thought of the phrase all the kids used. "I'll do my own thing!" she laughed to herself.

* * * *

When Millie had been with Fred and Jan for a week, Fred came home with the news. "I won! Pack your bags! We leave next Monday."

"But I can't leave Mother," Jan argued.

"I'll be fine. I think you should go," Millie said.

Jan finally agreed to the trip. Ginny Hendrix, a neighbor down the hall, promised to look after Millie.

Jan began to get excited about the trip. "It'll be like a second honeymoon."

"I hope so," Millie said. In her mind, she redid her bedroom as a nursery.

"Everything's going to be OK, George." Millie spoke softly as she rocked in her chair by the window.

Chapter 5

Millie was relieved when Jan dragged the last suitcase into the living room.

"Are you sure you'll be OK, Mother?" Jan asked.

"Of course, dear. Gertrude is visiting one day. And Ginny is right down the hall." Millie prayed that Jan wouldn't back out.

"Mom, how about helping me with this tie?" Fred was trying to fix a crooked knot. Millie began to fix it, but Jan took over. "Fred, I'll do it. Don't make work for Mother."

Millie wished Jan would calm down. She looked like a worried squirrel whose nuts were stolen.

"I really hate to leave you, Mother."

Millie accepted Jan's hug. "You're big enough to leave your mother. But neither one of you knows how to tie a tie. Fred's tie is still crooked."

"Thanks, Mom." Fred gave Millie a kiss when she straightened his tie. Then he carried the two large suitcases out the door. Jan followed with a smaller suitcase.

Millie bolted the door after them. Then she sat down to watch TV. *Life and Love* was just beginning. The camera was focused on Lucy. Maybe today Lucy would tell Don about the baby.

"Tell him, Lucy," Millie said aloud.

During a commercial, Millie went to her room to get her knitting.

She looked out the window. The bird woman was there in the park. One pigeon was pecking grains from her hand. Other birds came near enough to take the grains that had fallen on the ground.

Millie thought of the extra money she had put away. She had few needs. Fred didn't let her pay for gas or light. When Annie and Bill moved into her house, she'd have their rent money. Maybe she could help the bird woman. Or would it insult her?

Millie remembered the dollhouse for Jan's sixth birthday. Millie had saved two dollars a week from the household money. She was so proud to be able to give

Jan that dollhouse. She had made little curtains and stuffed chairs for it. It had all been hers. It hurt when George said, "Why did you do it? If I'd known, I could have bought that thing."

It bursts a bubble when people think they're doing real good and somebody says, "Let me help. I've got the money." It's like saying, "I can do it better." No, someday, she'd meet the bird woman. But she'd be careful about offering her things.

"Oh, Lord, you've got to have a better use for me than just staring out of this window. If I can't be with George, help me get rid of this self-pity. It's dumb and sinful. But that's how I feel. And without George, I don't know who I am."

As she thought of George, she began to cry. Through her tears, she watched the bird woman get up and hobble away.

Millie went back into the living room and turned off the TV. Then she went to the kitchen to fix herself some lunch. The cupboards were stocked with cans of soup. There was cold chicken and lunch meat in the refrigerator. As if I can't cook anymore, Millie thought.

As she was about to make a sandwich, there was a knock at the door.

"Mrs. Nelson. It's Ginny."

Millie unbolted the door.

"I'm sorry I'm so late. I promised Jan, but when I got home from work—"

"Come in and have some coffee. Can I make you a sandwich?"

"Jimmy's been a terror since I picked him up at the babysitter's. I can't think of where I am or what I'm doing. No, thank you anyway, but I can't stay."

"Maybe Jimmy would like to help me bake cookies."

"Jan wouldn't—"

"Jan wouldn't like it, but Jan isn't here," Millie said.

Jimmy appeared at the doorway. Dirty face, pout, and jelly bread in hand, he spoke. "Are you the old lady who lives here?"

Ginny's face flushed. But Millie chuckled. "I don't know. I live here."

Jimmy scratched his head and spread jelly to his hair.

"Did you have a good day at school?" Millie asked.

"No."

"Oh." Millie changed the subject. "I'm going to bake cookies. Think your mother could spare you to help?"

"Sure," he said. "How much do you pay?"

"Jimmy!" his mother said in shock.

Millie was confused. "Pay?"

"For helping with the cookies."

"Oh! Three cookies to eat here and six to take home. I'll even toss in a glass of milk if you help me wash the bowl," Millie promised.

"Do I get to lick it first?"

"Sure."

"It's a deal," Jimmy said.

"If it's OK with your mother." Millie looked at Ginny.

"Do you think you can handle him?"

Jimmy was pleased that his mother suggested he might be hard to handle.

"If my worker breaks our deal, I'll send him home."

Jimmy knew the lady meant it. He wouldn't do anything rotten. At least not until he got his cookies.

"Thank you, Mrs. Nelson. See you later," Ginny said.

"Call me Millie."

"Hey, Millie, let's get started," Jimmy said as she closed the door.

"Your *mother* may call me Millie. But you will call me Mrs. Nelson or Aunt Millie."

"I guess you're Aunt Millie."

Millie sent the boy off to wash his hands. When he came back, Millie patiently showed him how to blend the shortening and sugar. They measured the flour, salt, and baking soda.

While the cookies baked, Jimmy shared his troubles. "I hate school."

"Why?"

" 'Cause I got a dumb teacher," he said.

The boy reminded Millie of another small creature she once knew—her own Jan.

"Why do you say that?"

"She graded my paper wrong."

"Are you sure?"

"Yup."

"Maybe she made a mistake."

"Teachers shouldn't make mistakes."

"Do you make mistakes?"

"No—well, sometimes."

"I do, too."

"You do?" The boy looked at Millie with wide-eyed surprise.

"If we make mistakes, don't you think teachers should be allowed to?"

"I don't know."

"Why didn't you show her the paper?"

"I did. She said, 'Go back and sit down.' "

"Maybe if you talked nice."

"No way. She thinks I'm bad news."

"Do you make noise when she tries to have reading groups?"

"How did you know?"

"I didn't. But one of my friends was a teacher. That sort of thing bothered her. And when my girl was little—"

"Mrs. Beal?"

"Yes. She talked a lot when she wasn't supposed to."

"Wow! I didn't know that!"

"Now it doesn't give you an excuse to act that way. But sometimes, just knowing that somebody else had a problem helps."

Millie took the last batch of cookies from the oven. Jimmy drank his milk and ate his three cookies. As promised, Millie put six more cookies in a bag.

"Aw—do I have to go home now?"

"You can come back another day."

"Can I show you the paper the teacher goofed on?"

"OK."

Millie walked down the hall to Jimmy's apartment. She chatted with Ginny while the boy ran to get his paper. "Send Jimmy over again. We both had fun."

"We sure did," Jimmy said. "Aunt Millie, here's the paper."

"Oh, that again," Ginny sighed.

Millie looked at the paper. "Well, a perfect paper does deserve a star. His answer *is* right."

"She wouldn't listen to me," Jimmy complained. 'Go back and sit down.' That's all she said. I hate her."

"If your mother says its OK, how about the two of

us going to school in the morning?" Millie asked.

"I suppose I should go myself, " Ginny said, "But I have to work. Besides, I'm no good at handling things like this."

"Wow! Aunt Millie's gonna go to school and tell off old lady Bodner." Jimmy jumped up and down on the couch.

"Jimmy, sit down!" Ginny yelled.

"I'm not going to tell off your teacher, Jimmy," Millie said. "I just think we can clear up this misunderstanding."

"Get ready for bed, Jimmy." Ginny spoke firmly. After some argument, the boy trotted off.

"I don't know how to thank you, Mrs. Nelson," Ginny said.

"It's Millie, and the pleasure is all mine," Millie replied. "Now, what time is school?"

"It starts at nine o'clock. If you go with him, he'd better leave at eight-thirty."

Millie went back to her apartment. While Jan was away, it was *her* apartment. She listened to the news. No crashes of planes to Hawaii.

She checked the oven. Then she went to bed. For the first time since she moved in, it was easy to sleep.

Chapter 6

Jimmy knocked at the door five minutes early. Face, ears, and neck were clean. His clothes were spotless. His hair was slicked down. But a cowlick on top went its own way. His face glowed with a smile.

"Say, aren't you the handsome one," Millie said.

"I came early so you wouldn't have to walk fast."

"That was thoughtful."

"Aunt Millie, do you think the teacher's gonna be mad about you telling her off?"

"I'm not going to tell her off. I told you that before," Millie said.

"I wish you would," he said with a pout.

Jimmy had trouble slowing his pace on the way to school. He'd skip ahead a few steps. Then he'd bounce back a step.

At the door of the school, Millie told Jimmy to wait for the bell. Millie went inside. At the office, she met the principal, Mr. Jones.

She explained her mission. Mr. Jones took her to Mrs. Bodner's classroom. Jimmy had been wrong when he called her "old lady Bodner." The teacher was a tiny slip of a girl.

"That poor child," Mrs. Bodner said. "I'm sorry. He's just so active that— Oh, here I'm making excuses. It shouldn't have happened."

The bell rang.

"Jimmy," Mrs. Bodner said as Jimmy entered the room. "Jimmy, I'm very sorry for my mistake."

Jimmy looked at his shoes to avoid her eyes. "It's OK, I guess," he said.

"And thank you for bringing your friend. Would you like to introduce her to the class?"

Jimmy proudly addressed the class. "This is Aunt Millie," he said. "She'll let you call her Mrs. Nelson. But don't call her Millie. Only grown-ups can do that."

The class pledged to the flag. Then it was time to work. Children were everywhere. They rushed about the room. Mrs. Bodner was at the center of the action.

"No, Jane, page 16," she said. "I'll be around to help you in a minute."

"They all seem to need help at once," Millie observed.

"Some of the problems are little ones. An aide could help Charlie. He can add and subtract. But he can't tell a plus from a minus sign. The trouble is, the school doesn't have money for aides."

"My daughter had problems with signs. We made up a game about airplanes and submarines. But you probably have better ways."

"Not really," Mrs. Bodner sighed. "You don't suppose you would have time to help Charlie this morning?"

"Why, I'd love to," Millie said. "But I'm no teacher."

Before Millie could object anymore, Mrs. Bodner showed her the math.

"An airplane goes up—that's higher," Millie told Charlie. Soon he learned the game. Airplanes were plus. Submarines were minus.

Charlie taught his teacher the game.

"Amazing," said Mrs. Bodner. "Charlie, I think you've got it."

As Mrs. Bodner spoke, the music teacher came in. Millie and Mrs. Bodner walked down the hall together.

"Thank you. I had fun," Millie said.

"I should be thanking you," Mrs. Bodner said.

* * * *

The fall breeze whipped about with a damp chill. Winter was just around the corner. But Millie felt a warm glow. It was that special feeling when you know you're somebody—and you're a little proud of yourself.

Millie stopped at the coffee shop. There wasn't all that cigar smoke. But there weren't any people either. Coffee and pie aren't any fun without people, she thought. Besides, the crust was like cardboard. She couldn't eat it.

As Millie paid, the manager was direct. "Something wrong with the pie, lady?"

"No . . . I'm just used to my own crust. This was like— Well, it wasn't flaky."

"Like cardboard, maybe?" he asked.

Millie didn't like to complain. Avoiding any more talk, she took her change and hurried out.

"Sorry about that. Come again." The man spoke as Millie went out the door.

Nice man, Millie thought. But blunt.

Millie couldn't resist going into the pet store. A puppy in the window begged to be taken home. "Sorry, no pets allowed in my building," Millie said. Then she saw tanks of fish. Fish aren't pets, she reasoned.

She picked out a large bowl with two angel fish.

"You aren't planning to carry this far, are you?" the store owner asked. "The fish don't weigh much. But the bowl filled with water is almost impossible."

"Couldn't you empty the bowl and put the fish in a carton? I'll fill the bowl at home."

The man shook his head. "Tap water has to sit overnight. Otherwise, gases kill the fish."

"Oh. Well, I'll manage somehow," Millie said. "I only live over in Beldon Towers."

"I live over there, too! Tell you what. I'll deliver the fish this evening after I close."

Millie was filled with joy as she walked home. She had to tell someone about her morning. Ginny wouldn't be home for hours. So she called Gertrude.

After her phone call, she got a sheet and laid it over the TV. "Monster, you need a rest," she said aloud. She'd put the fish in her own room when Jan and Fred returned. But until then, watching them would replace TV.

The fish were delivered as promised. She put the bowl on top of the TV.

A little while later, the phone rang. It was Jan.

"Yes, I'm fine, dear," Millie said. "Don't worry—Yes, Ginny's been a big help."

Millie listened to Jan talk about the trip.

"Give my love to Fred, dear. And have a good time," Millie said before hanging up.

* * * *

"I haven't named my angel fish," Millie said as she turned out the lights. "Jimmy and Charlie would be nice."

Chapter 7

On Wednesday, while Gertrude was visiting, the school principal called.

"We don't want to impose," Mr. Jones said. "But you were so helpful. Could you come in one morning a week?"

Millie didn't even think twice about it. "I'd love to," she told him. She agreed to come in first thing Monday mornings.

On Thursday, she baked pies. She made one for herself, one for Ginny, one for the pet store owner, and one for the man at the coffee shop.

The owner of the pet shop was surprised.

The man at the coffee shop was speechless. He poured Millie a free cup of coffee. "Now this is what I call a pie," he said.

"Hey Mike," a customer said. "You can't do that to us. You take our good money for cardboard and stand there eating good stuff. It's been a month of Sundays since I had a good pie."

Mike felt he had to share his pie.

"This is the best cherry pie I've ever tasted," said the man. "You'd better hire the lady."

"Not a bad idea," Mike said. "Of course, the baking would have to be done here. State health rules."

"I couldn't. I promised the school I'd help them on Mondays. And my daughter wouldn't like it."

"Does your daughter run your life?"

"No."

"Then how about it? One day a week. It would be— What's your name?"

"Millie."

"OK. It would be Millie's Pie Day."

"I'll have to think about it," Millie said.

* * * *

In the old days, Friday had always been visiting day. So on Friday, Millie put on her coat and took off for the park. She hoped the bird woman wouldn't care

if she joined her. She didn't have any seeds, but maybe bread crusts would do.

"I've been watching you feed the birds," Millie said to the woman. "I hope you don't mind if I join you."

The woman was puzzled. She spoke a few words in another language. Millie guessed it was Spanish.

Millie sat next to the woman on the bench. She held out some crusts to her. The woman smiled and took the crusts. And together, they fed the birds.

I could be her friend, Millie thought. But isn't it a shame we can't talk to each other?

The woman pointed out a bird. Millie offered it a crust. It flew to her hand. At first, Millie was fearful. The beak was threatening. And the claws could pinch. But as the bird grabbed the food, Millie thanked the bird woman. The words were lost, but the woman nodded and smiled.

After the bird woman left, Millie stayed a while. She knitted. It was cold for knitting in the park. But it wasn't glove weather yet.

An out-of-breath jogger sat down beside her.

"What are you making?" the woman asked.

"A coat sweater for my daughter," Millie replied.

"My grandmother used to knit," the jogger said. "I loved to watch her when I was a child. I always wanted to learn, but she died when I was very young."

As they talked, Millie learned more about the young woman. Her name was Jill. She was a law student. And she was training to run in a marathon next month.

By the time Jill was ready to finish her run, they had made plans to get together again. Jill was going to come to Millie's apartment the next day for a knitting lesson.

After Jill jogged off, Millie started to pack up her knitting. The police officer came by and commented on Millie's knitting. Before too long, Millie had invited her to come over Saturday, too.

On the way home, Millie stopped at the pet shop. "I couldn't go home without seeing my friend." She spoke as she petted the little dog.

A woman was behind the counter. "I'll bet you're the woman my husband delivered the fish to," she said.

Millie laughed that she was.

"I hear we're neighbors," the woman said. They promised to spend some time together soon.

* * * *

After lunch, Millie took a nap. Later, she did other visiting on the phone. Gertrude told her that Annie and Bill hadn't moved in yet.

Jill called later to ask if she could bring a friend with her tomorrow morning.

About four, there was a knock. It was Sara Henson, from the pet shop. Millie invited her to come over in the morning, too.

After Sara left, tomorrow's importance occurred to Millie. She would be giving a party. It would be the first party in her new home. It would make the apartment more of a home for her. And that called for baking and cleaning.

Jimmy came by after school as he now did every day. Millie put him to work.

"I don't know how to dust," he complained.

"Now's the time to learn," Millie told him. He dusted everything twice to please Aunt Millie.

Ginny came down to get him for dinner.

"I'm working, Mom," Jimmy announced.

"I'm impressed," Ginny said.

"We're getting ready for a knitting party," Millie told her. "Want to come?"

That brought the number of guests to five.

The phone rang while Ginny was there.

"Yes, Jan," Millie said. She looked at Ginny as she spoke. "Ginny is taking care of me. In fact, she's here right now. How's Hawaii?"

Millie listened to the voice at the other end. "Oh, don't cut the trip short. You both need time to relax."

After the phone call, Millie tried to think about the party. But she couldn't help worrying about Jan.

Her grief's still so bottled up, George, Millie thought. She loved you so.

Then Millie thought of her new freedom. She had let George take care of her all their years together. Being taken care of was safe and easy, even if she had resented it sometimes. But now, she was excited about being on her own and being her own person. She couldn't give it up when Jan returned. And that worried her.

Chapter 8

Some of the attempts at knitting were awkward. But the party was a great success. The women talked as they knitted.

"I love my work," Jill said. "But my parents are pushing me. They want me to forget about becoming a lawyer. They say I owe it to my husband to have a baby. I don't understand it. There are so many unwanted babies in the world. You'd think this thing of motherhood for all would end."

"Doesn't your husband want a child?" Millie asked.

"Not now. Our careers are our lives. But my parents take some of the joy out of my success. It's awful to be put down when you succeed."

Millie's eyes moved to the prize still-life over the sofa. Embarrassed, she thought about how she had told Jan that a baby would be nicer than that art award. Our sins speak louder from a stranger's tongue, she thought.

When the party was in full swing, the door flew open. In walked Jan. Behind her was Fred.

"J-Jan. Welcome home, dear." Millie hugged her daughter, who stood cold and stunned.

"We didn't expect you so soon. You just called last night," Millie said.

"I didn't tell you then, Mother. I was calling from the airport. Hawaii's a fun place. But a few days were all I could take."

"Jan, I want you to meet my friends. You know Ginny, of course. This is Jill. She's a law student. And Lila is Jill's neighbor. You've probably seen Pat in the park. She's a police officer. And Sara lives right downstairs. She and her husband own the pet store down the street. That's where I got Charlie and Jimmy."

"Who?" Jan was confused.

"The angel fish. Aren't they cute?"

Jan gasped as she caught sight of the covered TV and the fish bowl.

"But Mom! How did you watch TV?"

"I didn't, dear. The fish were more interesting. Besides, I didn't have time to watch much TV. But don't you worry. I was going to have Fred put the bowl on my nightstand."

Fred was laughing. "You've really been living it up, haven't you, Mom?"

Ginny was the only guest aware of Jan's mood. Jan remained polite, but cool, until all the guests but Ginny had left.

Then Jan lashed forth. "What was going on here?" she screamed.

"Just a little party, dear," Millie said calmly.

"You invited *strangers* into *my* home?"

Millie was silent for a moment. She had thought of the party as a way to make the place *her* home, too. But it seemed Jan saw her as a guest.

Millie finally answered her daughter. "They're my friends, not strangers."

"And just where did you meet them? Picked them up in the park, I suppose," Jan shouted.

Ginny slipped out the door. Millie glanced at her apologetically.

"Jan, cool it." Fred was angry. "If Mom's going to live here, she has a right to friends and get-togethers."

"They're all half her age! Why doesn't she act her age? She should have been resting," Jan argued.

"Seems one gets enough of that in the grave," Millie answered.

"And you're in a hurry to get there," Jan shouted.

"Well you seem to think I *already* have one foot in the grave," Millie exploded.

"Jan—" Fred started to say.

"Oh, you don't understand," Jan said angrily. She dragged a suitcase into the bedroom.

Millie took a deep breath and followed her daughter into the bedroom.

"Jan, we have to talk," Millie said. "I can't hold back my feelings anymore to spare you. It doesn't help either one of us."

Jan slammed a drawer in reply. But Millie kept on talking. She told Jan about helping out at the school. To Jan, the idea was absurd.

"Mom, you're too old," she said. "If the kids need help, let their parents do it."

The coffee shop job was even more upsetting to Jan. She yelled, "You can't do it!"

Millie said, "Yes I can. Now sit down. Listen to me. I can't take any more of your pushing. From now on, I make my own decisions."

"But—" Jan started to argue.

"No, wait a minute. I'm not finished, Jan. I also think I should be thinking about getting a place of my own. I don't want to be your *guest* for the rest of my life."

Millie didn't know where she was getting the courage to say what she was saying. She was letting out all the feelings that had built up these many weeks since George died.

"Mom," Jan said in shock. "Who will look after you?"

"I will. I'm the only one who should be looking after me. Jan, get busy with your painting. Take your studio back. You and Fred tend to *your* lives. *I'll* tend to mine. Only God has the right to be everybody's boss."

Jan started to cry.

Fred had been standing in the doorway. He came over and gently put his arm around his wife. "Mom's right. You haven't let her live her own life."

"I was just keeping my promise to Daddy," Jan sobbed.

"Promise?" Millie asked.

"When he was dying. It was the last time I saw him alive. He said, 'Jan, promise to take care of Millie. She isn't used to deciding things for herself.' "

Millie looked to the sky and spoke. "George Nelson, if you can hear me up there, take a listen. I loved you. I loved you so much that I put up with your

bossing. But I'm not as helpless as we both thought. You're not here now, and I won't be bossed. *I'll* decide what's right for me."

Jan wiped her eyes. "I'm sorry, Mom. I was just trying to take care of you. Daddy was so worried about you."

Millie comforted her daughter. "This has been a hard time for all of us. And we were all walking around like bombs ready to go off. Now we've exploded. I hope we can be more honest with each other from now on."

Jan started to cry again. She cried for many hours. Then she fell asleep. Millie covered her with a blanket.

* * * *

The real estate agent called the next day. Annie and Bill had called off their wedding. No rental.

"Now I guess you'll move back home, Mom?" Jan said when she heard the news.

"No." Millie paused. "But I thought you and Fred might move there. You need more space for your artwork. The new thruway is almost finished. It would be easy for Fred to drive to work. I thought maybe I could sublet this place from you."

Millie went on. "I think I need to live alone for a while. I need to do for myself. Besides, I'm starting a new life here. My friends, the school, my pie day at the coffee shop—"

Millie paused and looked at Jan. Jan still wasn't happy about that last part. But she smiled weakly anyway.

****

Most of the tension was gone now. Jan eagerly planned their move.

"Mom, do you mind if I turn the upstairs into an art studio?"

"Of course not, dear. It will be your home again. Do whatever you want."

Millie was eagerly making plans, too. There were many new things she wanted to do. She was even thinking of taking a Spanish course so she could talk to the bird woman.

Millie was scared, too, about all the changes in her life. But she had misplaced a part of herself during her years with George. And she wasn't going to let it happen again with Jan.

"For 40 years, I've been somebody's wife or somebody's mother," Millie said to her daughter. "Now I'm going to be Millie Nelson. And *I'm* going to take care of me."